SOAP SOAP SOAP
Jabón Jabón Jabón

Words and Pictures by ~
Palabras y dibujos de

Elizabeth O. Dulemba

*For Stan (always),
Olivia and Hughlito.*

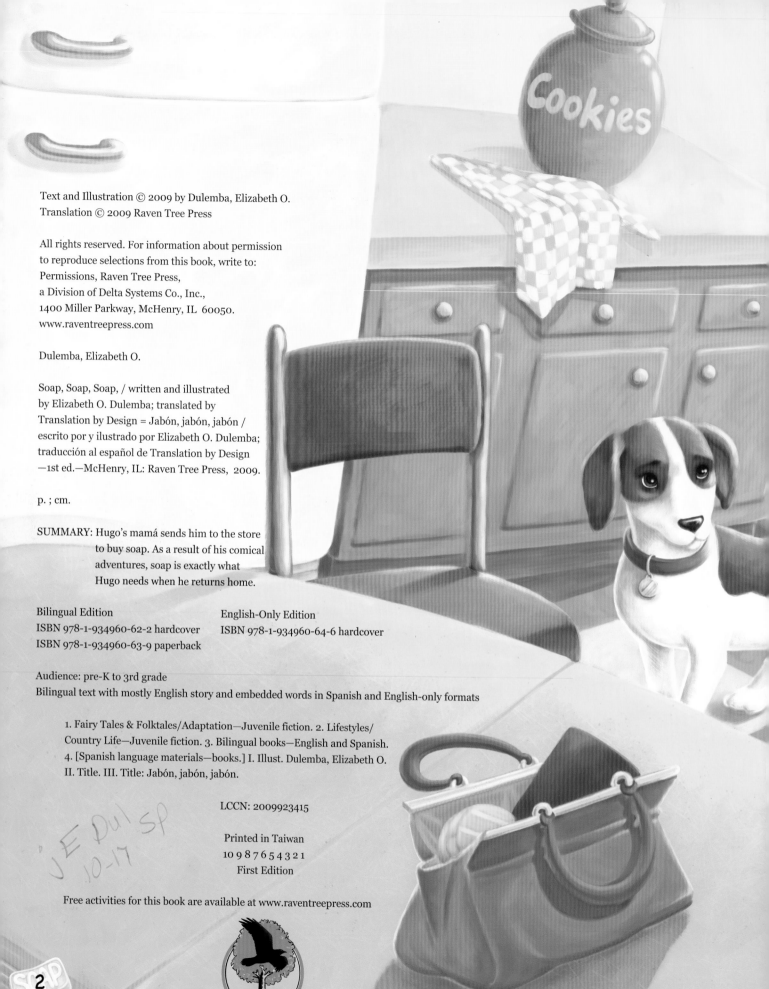

Dulemba, Elizabeth O.

Soap, Soap, Soap, / written and illustrated
by Elizabeth O. Dulemba; translated by
Translation by Design = Jabón, jabón, jabón /
escrito por y ilustrado por Elizabeth O. Dulemba;
traducción al español de Translation by Design
—1st ed.—McHenry, IL: Raven Tree Press, 2009.

p. ; cm.

SUMMARY: Hugo's mamá sends him to the store
to buy soap. As a result of his comical
adventures, soap is exactly what
Hugo needs when he returns home.

Bilingual Edition
ISBN 978-1-934960-62-2 hardcover
ISBN 978-1-934960-63-9 paperback

English-Only Edition
ISBN 978-1-934960-64-6 hardcover

Audience: pre-K to 3rd grade
Bilingual text with mostly English story and embedded words in Spanish and English-only formats

1. Fairy Tales & Folktales/Adaptation—Juvenile fiction. 2. Lifestyles/
Country Life—Juvenile fiction. 3. Bilingual books—English and Spanish.
4. [Spanish language materials—books.] I. Illust. Dulemba, Elizabeth O.
II. Title. III. Title: Jabón, jabón, jabón.

LCCN: 2009923415

Printed in Taiwan
10 9 8 7 6 5 4 3 2 1
First Edition

Free activities for this book are available at www.raventreepress.com

Raven Tree Press
A Division of Delta Systems Co., Inc.
www.raventreepress.com

"Hugo, please run to the store for me," his mamá said as she handed him some money. "Here's some dinero. We need soap. Go straight to the store and buy jabón."

3

But Hugo's path to the store was
across the playground,
down the sidewalk, and
beyond the ditch that ran by his school.
Hugo wanted to remember what he
needed to buy, so all the way to
el mercado he said,
"soap, soap, soap! ¡jabón, jabón, jabón!"

4

Hugo was near the playground when
he slipped in a puddle of mud.

Kersploosh!

His slide through the charco de barro surprised
Hugo so much that he forgot what his mother
wanted him to buy at el mercado.

Hugo stood frowning at the charco de barro. He walked to the left of the mud puddle. "Here I remembered."

He walked to the right. "There I forgot."

Just then Hugo's neighbor, Jellybean Jones, walked by. She said, "If you tell me what you're looking for, I'll help you find it."

"I don't know!" Hugo replied.
"Aquí I remembered.
Allí I forgot."

"You're a funny boy, Hugo. And muddy too!"
Jellybean said as she hurried by. And then . . .

Jellybean also slipped in the charco de barro.

Kersploosh!

"Whoa," she said. "The mud is as slippery as soap!"
Suddenly Hugo remembered and shouted "¡jabón!"

Jellybean yelled, "Now I'm muddy
too and it's your fault!"
"Lo siento. I'm sorry,"
Hugo said as he ran away.
But then he had "lo siento" stuck in his
head and he forgot all about the soap.

Hugo was still repeating "lo siento" when he passed Señora Soto on the sidewalk. She had dropped her grocery bag and broken the eggs. Huevos *oozed* everywhere.

She overheard Hugo saying "lo siento" and blamed him for the mess. "Joven," she said, "Young man, I'm out of eggs, so you are in . . ."

13

Hugo didn't hear the rest.
He wriggled free and took off running.
But now he had "I'm out, so you are in"
stuck in his cabeza.
And he still could not remember what
his mother wanted him to buy at el mercado.

Hugo started to jump over the ditch that ran by his school.
He didn't see Bubba down in la zanja.
But the bully heard Hugo say, "I'm out, so you are in."

Bubba yelled, "I'll show you who's in!"
and pulled Hugo into la zanja.

EAST
SIDE
ELEMENTARY

Just then Principal Vargas arrived on the scene.
"¡Basta! Stop! Break this up!" he said and sent Bubba home.
"¡Por Dios! My goodness! Hugo, you're a mess.
You need a bath. Un baño with lots of soap!"
Suddenly Hugo remembered and shouted, "¡jabón!"

Now Hugo was muddy *and* stinky too,
but he still had to go to el mercado.
To help him remember what he
needed to buy, Hugo kept repeating

Soap, soap, soap!
¡jabón, jabón, jabón!

Señor Sanchez, the Grocer, said,
"Oye, Hugo, what would you like?"
Hugo smiled and said,
"soap, soap, soap! ¡jabón, jabón, jabón!"
"¡Claro!" Señor Sanchez said. "Of course!"

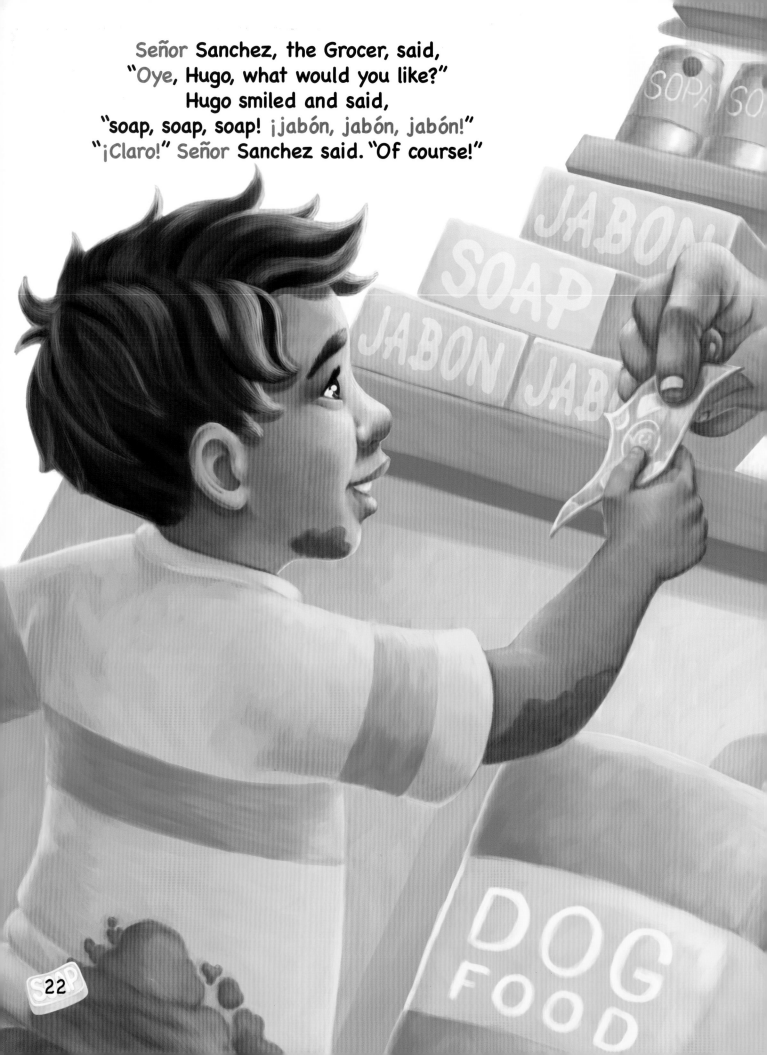

Hugo handed Señor Sanchez
el dinero and finally got the soap.
"Thank you! ¡Gracias!" Hugo said as he ran
out the door and back toward his home.

This time he jumped over la zanja.

He dodged around Señora Soto who was still complaining about the huevos.

And he hurried across the playground,
but walked very, very slowly
past the charco de barro. Muy, muy lento.

When Hugo returned home, his mamá was
happy to see him—but not the mud.
"¡Por Dios! My goodness!" she cried.
"Hugo, you're a mess. You need un baño!
It's no wonder we use so much soap!"

26

Hugo's mamá took him by the sleeve
and marched him to the tub . . .

. . . where she made him
scrub, scrub, scrub with
jabón, jabón, jabón!

31

Vocabulario / Vocabulary

jabón = soap

mamá = mother

el dinero = money

el mercado = market

¡Ay, caramba! = Whoa!

charco de barro =

puddle of mud

aquí = here

allí = there

Lo siento = I'm sorry

Señora = Mrs.

huevos = eggs

joven = young man

cabeza = head

la zanja = ditch

¡Basta! = Stop!

¡Por Dios! = My goodness!

un baño = a bath

Señor = Mr.

oye = listen

claro = of course

gracias = thank you

muy, muy lento =

very, very slowly